49p

Hodder Toddler

This book belongs to:

Madeleine .... from ....

St. Thomas pre-school   2002

To Maisie and Clem
with love from mummy

To Emer and Cormac AE

ONE TOO MANY TIGERS
Written by Cressida Cowell
Illustrated by Andy Ellis

British Library Cataloguing in Publication Data
A catalogue record of this book is available from the British Library.

ISBN 0 340 79214 0 (PB)

First edition published 2001
10 9 8 7 6 5 4 3

Published by Hodder Children's Books,
a division of Hodder Headline Limited,
338 Euston Road, London NW1 3BH

Printed in Hong Kong

One Too Many Tigers

Written by Cressida Cowell
Illustrated by Andy Ellis

Hodder
Children's
Books

A division of Hodder Headline Limited

One was Tootle
and Tootle was a tiger.

One sleepy tiger in the Tiger Tree.

Two was Mummy
and Mummy was a tiger too.

Two sleepy tigers in the Tiger Tree.

TIGER
TREE

Three was Daddy
and Daddy was a tiger too.

Three *sleepy* tigers in the Tiger Tree.

Four was Titbit
and Titbit was a tiger too . . .

TIGER
TREE

'Hang on a minute,' said Tootle.
'There are **ONE TOO MANY TIGERS**
in the Tiger Tree.'

'Leaping leopards!' said Daddy Tiger.

'Jumping jaguars!' said Mummy Tiger.

'WHATEVER SHALL WE DO?'

'Follow me,' said Cockatoo,
'and remember the old tiger saying:

When the number of tails is
more than three . . .

. . . you need to find a bigger tree!'

So Daddy Tiger went to sleep on FOUR big branches...

And Mummy Tiger went to sleep on three medium-sized branches...

And Tootle Tiger went to sleep on two small branches...

And Titbit Tiger went to sleep on one teeny-weeny little branch...

And there weren't TOO MANY TIGERS after all.

OR WERE THERE?

Goodbye
Hodder Toddler